Behind the
Locked Door

Behind the Locked Door

Paul McCusker

PUBLISHING
Colorado Springs, Colorado

BEHIND THE LOCKED DOOR

Copyright © 1993 by Focus on the Family

Library of Congress Cataloging-in-Publication Data
McCusker, Paul,   1958–
        Behind the locked door / Paul McCusker.
            p.   cm. — (Adventures in Odyssey ; 4)
        Summery: Mark's curiosity leads him into trouble when he stays with Mr.
Whittaker, the owner of Whit's End, while his mother is in Washington, D.C., trying
to work out differences with Mark's father.
        ISBN 1-56179-133-4
        [1. Conduct of life—Fiction. 2. Divorce—Fiction.]   I. Title.   II Series:
McCusker, Paul,   1958–   Adventure in Odyssey ;   4.
PZ7.M47841635Be   1993
[Fic]—dc20   93-1749
                                                                                                                          CIP
                                                                                                                          AC

Published by Focus on the Family Publishing, Colorado Springs, CO 80920.

Distributed in the U.S.A. and Canada by Word Books, Dallas, Texas.

Editors: Deena Davis and Larry K. Weeden
Interior illustrations: Jeff Stoddard
Interior design: Tim Howard
Cover illustration: Jeff Haynie

Printed in the United States of America

   94 95 96 97/10 9 8 7 6 5 4 3 2

for Phil Lollar —
friend and fellow adventurer

Fans of the audio and video series of
Adventures in Odyssey *may wonder why some*
of their favorite characters aren't found in these
novels. The answer is simple: the novels take
place in a period of time prior to the audio
or video series.

Contents

CHAPTER ONE

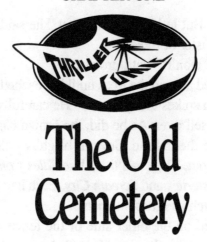

The Old Cemetery

Mark Prescott stopped, pushed his dark hair back from his forehead, and looked up at the sky. The August sun ducked behind black and purple clouds. It had been playing hide-and-seek for a week now.

"It's going to rain," Mark said, resuming his stroll with Patti Eldridge.

Patti pulled her baseball cap down tighter on her head, as if bracing for an immediate downpour. Her blue eyes peered at Mark from the shadow of its brim. "Let's run back to my house," she said.

Mark nodded and shoved a flat, brown bag under his light

1

jacket. "Okay. But let's take a shortcut," he said and bolted into a small cluster of trees.

"No, Mark! Don't!" Patti protested.

Mark dodged around the trees until he reached a wrought-iron fence with spikes along the top. He carefully climbed it and threw himself over. As he did, the brown bag fell out of his jacket onto the ground. Several brightly colored comic books slipped out. They had titles like *Tales from the Tomb*, *Forbidden Mysteries*, and *Scream City*. Each had a menacing drawing to match its gruesome name.

Patti stopped on the other side of the fence while Mark picked up the comic books. "I don't know why you buy those things," she said.

Mark ignored her and slipped them back into the brown bag.

"Seriously, Mark! They're disgusting," she continued. "You'll warp your mind reading stuff like that."

Mark dismissed her comments with a wave of his hand. "Girls don't know anything about it," he said.

Patti glared at him.

He looked away. He knew it was an unfair thing to say to her. Since his arrival in Odyssey after his parents separated, Mark had found Patti to be a good friend. The fact that she was a girl bothered him at first. Boys didn't have girls as friends. At least, that's what he thought. But she remained friendly to him, even after he was impatient and rude to her.

In time, after several adventures together, he realized it

didn't matter if she was a girl. He stopped thinking about it altogether—except when someone would tease them for being together so much or when Patti would do something he considered "girl-like." For example, she expected a compliment when she wore a new dress, and sometimes she would say that another boy was "cute."

"What do you mean, girls don't know anything about it?" Patti asked.

"Never mind," he said and turned to walk on. "Let's go."

"Oh, really?" she said, frowning at him.

Mark looked back at her with a blank expression. He thought she was going to nag him about the comic books some more, but then he realized she had something else on her mind.

"Well? How am I supposed to get over?" she finally asked.

Mark suddenly realized what the problem was. He had forgotten that Patti's right arm was in a plaster cast. She had broken it a few weeks before after falling into an abandoned mine shaft inside a cave. That was one adventure Mark was ashamed to think about. The cave was her secret hideout, and he had told people about it after promising not to. Although Patti never brought it up after he apologized to her, he felt she still blamed him. *Why wouldn't she?* Mark often thought. I'd *be mad if she betrayed* me.

"There's a gate over that way," Mark mumbled. They walked along together on opposite sides of the fence.

Patti sighed. "Look, all I'm saying is that you're gonna get in big trouble with your mom if she ever finds out you spent your whole allowance on those sick books!"

"But she *won't* find out unless someone blabs," Mark replied.

Patti frowned. "Nobody has to blab. They're going to get you in trouble all by themselves."

"Quit nagging me!" Mark shouted.

They reached the gate in silence. A dark feeling hung over them just like one of the rain clouds above.

Patti walked through the gate. "You didn't have to shout at me," she said.

Mark lowered his tone and replied, "Yeah, I know. Just drop it, okay?" It was the closest thing to an apology he could manage.

There wasn't anything else to say, so they walked on. Mark wondered how long it would take her to realize where they were. The thick grove of trees gave no clue, nor did the perfectly trimmed carpet of grass that cushioned their walk. But after a moment the trees gave way to a clearing, and the carpet of grass stretched before them dotted with gray, eroded tombstones covered with dark moss.

They were in the graveyard next to Saint Patrick's, Odyssey's oldest church.

Patti stopped in her tracks. "Oh no . . ."

"Oh, come on, Patti. It's just a graveyard," Mark said.

"I know it's a graveyard," Patti snapped. "Let's go around."

Mark shook his head. "Why go all the way around? It's a great shortcut! I found it the other day when I went to your house from Whit's End."

"I don't like it," said Patti.

Mark quickened his step. "We'll only be here a minute. Come on."

"I don't like it," Patti said again, wrinkling her freckled nose. But she followed Mark anyway.

They wove along the edge of the tombstones. Mark normally would have walked right through the center, but he didn't think Patti would dare. Her eyes, wide with fright, darted back and forth as if she expected a hand to suddenly reach out and grab her.

They were closer to the church now. It was a large building of sandy-colored stones fashioned like the old cathedrals Mark had seen in pictures. Washington, D.C., where Mark had lived before he moved to Odyssey, had a cathedral. It was bigger than this church, but it had the same kind of tower that jutted high into the sky. It even had working bells. Mark had never heard the bells ring in this Odyssey church.

"Hurry up," Patti whispered.

But Mark was in no hurry. He wanted to see some of the names and dates etched in the tombstones beneath small crosses and statues of angels' wings. "Beloved son" . . . "Joshua David Penrose, 1877-1898" . . . "In the arms of

Jesus" . . . "Victoria Simpson, 1860-1922." *They were all people who once lived like me*, Mark thought. *They went shopping and took shortcuts and jumped fences and . . .*

Patti suddenly gasped. "Look!"

Mark followed her gaze. Off in the distance, across the collection of weathered stones, Mark saw John Avery Whittaker leaning over a grave. Everyone in town knew John Whittaker—or Whit, as he was best known. He owned a remarkable ice cream parlor called Whit's End that housed room after room of activities and displays for kids. "A discovery emporium," Mark heard some people call it. Kids could run the county's largest train set, perform on the stage in the Little Theatre, read through any of the hundreds of books in the library, or build an invention in the workroom.

Mark had experienced his share of adventures in and around Whit's End, including one with a time machine called the Imagination Station. He liked to think he and Whit were good friends. But he suspected Whit made all the kids feel that way.

"He's putting flowers on a grave!" Patti whispered.

"I wonder whose grave it is," Mark said, craning his neck to get a better look. The sight of Whit in a graveyard stirred a strong feeling of curiosity inside Mark. It reminded him of a story in one of his comic books about a ghost dressed in black who waited next to a grave for a woman who would never arrive.

Drops of rain lightly spattered Mark and Patti. They only

had time to look up before the sky gave way to a full-fledged downpour.

"I want to go home," Patti said. She moved to the shelter of a tree. Mark was a few steps behind her, but he kept his eyes on Whit.

"Did you hear me?" asked Patti.

Through the dull gray rain, Mark watched as Whit stepped back from the grave and slowly lowered his head. His white hair, normally wild and seemingly alive, lay matted against his forehead. Even his bushy, white eyebrows and mustache drooped under the weight of the falling water. After a moment, he turned and walked off in the opposite direction.

"It's as if he doesn't even know it's raining," Mark said.

"Well *I* do!" Patti complained.

"I want to know whose grave that is," Mark said as he took a step in that direction.

Patti grabbed his arm. "No, Mark. Let's get out of here. This place gives me the creeps!"

"There's nothing to be afraid of," said Mark.

"I don't care," Patti replied. "I'm not supposed to get my cast wet!"

Mark frowned and jerked his thumb at her cast. "You just don't want to mess up all those stupid autographs you got from everybody at Whit's End."

"So?"

"So—if you had left Whit's End when I wanted to, we wouldn't be caught in the rain now," Mark asserted.

Patti's mouth fell open. "I can't believe you! You're not going to blame this on me. Getting people to sign my cast is the only thing that makes it bearable!"

"I just want to see the tombstone," he pleaded. "I'll only be a minute."

Patti was about to answer when suddenly a haggard, old man appeared from behind a nearby tree. "Hey!" he shouted.

Mark and Patti cried out.

The rain had smeared dirt on the man's craggy face. His clothes were unkempt and torn. Mark thought of the cover of one of his horror comic books—a drawing of a corpse emerging from a fresh grave.

The old man stepped toward them and waved his fist. "This ain't no playground!" he shouted.

Mark and Patti ran for their lives.

CHAPTER TWO

A Sudden Announcement

Once they were a safe distance away, Mark and Patti slowed down to catch their breath in the shelter of a covered bus stop. The rain falling against the roof sounded like a beating drum.

"I told you we shouldn't cut through there!" Patti shouted above the roar.

"It was just some old man," Mark said, then laughed. "You thought it was a monster."

Patti looked at him doubtfully. "Oh yeah? If you thought it was just some old man, why did *you* run?"

"Because *you* ran," Mark replied.

"You were scared," said Patti.

"No more than you were," said Mark. They argued back and forth about who was more scared until it was obvious no one could win the argument.

"I'm going home now," Patti said. "My mom's gonna have a fit when she sees how wet I am."

Mark caught Patti's sleeve just as she was about to dash into the rain. "Whose grave do you think Whit was visiting?"

Patti turned to him impatiently. "I don't know, and I don't think it's any of our business, Mark. It's not right to spy on people in graveyards."

"Aren't you even a little bit curious?" Mark asked.

Patti didn't answer, but her expression told Mark she was. She held her cast close to her chest, lowered her head, and charged into the downpour. Before long, she disappeared into the watery haze.

Mark strolled out of the shelter as if it weren't raining at all. Getting wet didn't bother him. Not when his mind was on Whit. What was he doing in that cemetery? Whose grave was it? Patti had lived in Odyssey a long time. Why didn't she know? Why hadn't Mark heard that Whit knew someone buried there?

The questions swirled round and round in his brain like water down a drain. But there were no answers to be found. It only made him realize how little he knew about Whit. The pleasant and wise owner of Whit's End was now a man of mystery.

Mark threw open the front door to his house and stepped in. "Mom?" he called out. No reply. He took two steps and almost forgot to take off his shoes. His mom would have been angry if he had tracked mud on the carpet. He absent-mindedly tugged off his shoes and dropped them next to the mat. He then pulled off his jacket, hung it up, and inspected his comic books. They were damp but not drenched.

"Mom!" Mark called again, wondering where she was. The loud ticking of the grandfather clock in the hall was the only response to his call. His socks made squishing sounds as he padded upstairs to his bedroom and threw the comic books into the top drawer of his dresser. A ghoulish face leered at him as he closed the drawer. Patti's words came back to him. One day, those comic books were going to get him in trouble.

He shrugged off the thought and ran back downstairs to the kitchen. As he reached for the refrigerator door to get a drink, he discovered a note stuck under a plastic magnet shaped like a cuddly kitten. The refrigerator was covered with those kinds of magnets. Mark thought they looked sissy.

"Don't go anywhere. Important news," the note said in his mother's handwriting. *Now what?* Mark wondered. He closed his eyes and took a deep breath. Ever since his mother and father had separated, Mark had prepared himself for all kinds of "news." First, it was his mother's news that they were leaving their home in Washington, D.C., to move to Odyssey. Then it was the news that his mother and father were getting a divorce. Then they had changed their minds and wanted to try to make their marriage work. Then it was the news that working out their problems would be a long and slow process. Maybe adults understood such things, but Mark sometimes felt as if he were on a roller coaster. All he could do was close his eyes and wait for the butterflies to stop flapping their wings in his stomach. Mostly he wished the ride would end and they could be a family again.

"News," Mark whispered to himself. He had no way of predicting whether the news would be good or bad. His parents had been talking on the phone a lot lately. Sometimes Mark's mom seemed excited; other times, she hung up the phone in tears. He never asked about it. He figured the answer would be more than he'd want to know.

The electric garage door opener suddenly groaned to life. In his mind's eye, Mark could see what his ears told him was happening. The car hummed and hissed its way into place. The brakes squeaked, and the motor cut off. With a loud click, the door opened. A soft dong-dong-dong announced that Julie Prescott needed to take the keys out of the ignition. Mark then heard some shuffling of paper bags—*probably groceries,* he thought—and went to the door leading into the garage. He opened it in time for his mother to step through with two large bags in her arms. They weren't groceries.

"Close the car door, sweetheart," she said breathlessly.

Mark obeyed and returned in seconds. His mom was still in her dripping raincoat as she carefully pulled a pink blouse from the bag. She held it up and smiled.

"Hi," he said.

"Hi," she replied. "What do you think?"

Mark shrugged. He couldn't decide if he wanted to press her for the news or wait until she chose to tell him.

Julie draped the blouse over the back of a kitchen chair. "Did you see my note?"

"Uh huh," Mark said.

"I suppose you're wondering what the news is." She smiled.

Mark rolled his eyes. *I hope she isn't going to make me guess*, he thought.

She pushed him playfully. "Don't roll your eyes at me, young man. Otherwise I won't tell you."

"Mom!" Mark cried out, putting his hands on his hips.

"That's better," she said. She took off her raincoat and left it to drip on a coat rack next to the garage door.

"So?"

Running her fingers through her damp, brown hair, she leaned forward to face Mark. Her hazel eyes danced. "I talked to your father today, and we decided I should go back to Washington for a few days. There's a counselor he wants us to see. I'll catch a flight tomorrow. This could be it, Mark."

" 'It'?" Mark blinked.

His mom pushed a loose strand of hair away from her

face. "If the counseling goes well, your father and I might . . . might . . . you know . . . *reconcile.*"

The word didn't mean anything to Mark. Suddenly his mother realized it and said, "That means we'll get back together. We'll be a *family* again!"

Mark's heart jumped, but he told it to be still. He knew better than to get excited about this announcement. He'd heard such statements before. "But what about me?" he asked.

"Is that all you can say? Aren't you pleased?" Julie's mouth fell open with disbelief. It was her turn to put her hands on her hips.

Mark shrugged again. "I was just wondering where I'll stay while you're gone."

"I'll never figure you out. I thought you'd be happy." She went back to the bags and pulled out a charcoal skirt.

"I *am* happy," Mark said. "But you and Dad have been doing this *forever*. He comes here and you get counseling, or you go there and get counseling, and then you say you need more time and nothing happens."

Julie stopped digging in the bags and turned to Mark. "You're right," she said softly, reaching out to stroke his hair. "It's not fair to expect you to jump for joy every time something like this comes up. But it really is different now. You'll see."

Mark gazed down at his socks and wiggled his toes uncomfortably. The bottoms of his jeans were wet.

"I have some other news, too," she said.

Other news? Mark looked up at her. "What other news?"

"I arranged for you to stay with someone while I'm away."

At Patti's, I'll bet, Mark thought.

Julie's voice rose excitedly as she said, "You're going to stay at Mr. Whittaker's house!"

CHAPTER THREE

A Mysterious Door

W hile Julie packed for the trip, Mark called Patti to tell her the news. She screamed into the phone so loudly that Mark had to hold the receiver away from his ear. "You're staying at Whit's *house?* You're staying at his *house?* You are going to stay at his own personal *house?*" she asked.

He wanted to sound casual, but he was pleased with her reaction. "Yeah, Mom's taking me first thing tomorrow," he said.

"Wow! I don't know *anyone* who's ever been inside Whit's *house!*"

Mark shrugged, even though she couldn't see it. He knew it was an honor to go to Whit's.

"I have some news, too," Patti said, lowering her voice. "I told my parents about seeing Whit at the graveyard."

"Why did you do that?" Mark asked sharply.

"Because I thought they might know something about it," Patti retorted.

Mark softened his tone. "What did they say?"

Patti hesitated, and for a moment Mark thought she might not tell him because he had spoken harshly. Then she said, "They think it might be Jenny Whittaker's grave. She died a couple of years ago."

Whit was married? Mark closed his eyes and tried to picture it. *Of course he was. Why wouldn't he be?* Yet, it was hard for Mark to imagine the Whit he knew having a wife and doing the kinds of things married people do. He just couldn't see it.

"Hello? Mark?"

"How did she die?" Mark finally asked.

"My folks weren't sure," Patti answered. She went on to explain she didn't want to press them with too many questions or they might lecture her about minding her own business.

Like you lectured me, Mark thought.

"Anyway, I have to go," Patti said. "See you tomorrow."

"Okay, thanks," Mark said as he hung up the phone. His stomach flip-flopped. Suddenly he was full of all the anticipation he often felt on Christmas Eve. He knew he wouldn't sleep well that night.

From the doorway to his room, Mark stifled a shriek. His mother was opening his dresser drawers. *The comic books!* he remembered. "Mom!" he called out just as Julie reached for the drawer containing them.

Startled, Julie looked up at him. "What's wrong?"

"I, uh, was . . . " Mark swallowed hard. "I was just talking to Patti. She's excited that I'm staying with Whit."

"Good. But you didn't have to shout like that," Julie said. She turned to Mark's bed, where his carrying case lay open like the mouth of a baby bird screeching for a worm. Julie fed it some of Mark's underwear, then looked around uncertainly. "I don't want to forget anything."

Mark was afraid she might reach for the drawer again. He stepped in front of it as if he merely wanted to lean against the dresser and folded his arms casually.

"What's wrong with you?" Julie asked.

"Huh?"

"You're acting very strange," she said, eyeing him warily.

"I'm just . . . you know," he replied.

Julie gently put her hands on his shoulders. "I know it's hard, Mark. All this going back and forth between your father and me . . . it seems crazy sometimes. I know it does. If I were you, I'd think we were the worst parents in the world."

"You are not!" Mark said defensively.

"Well, hang in there," she said with a smile. "Your father

and I will meet with the counselor for two days of pretty tough talking. Then we'll decide if the time is right. Maybe this will be the happy ending we've all been praying for."

Mark didn't dare hope.

Julie kissed him on the cheek. "Take a look around to see if there's anything else you want to pack. I'll go downstairs and get us some lemonade."

She walked out of the room and down the stairs. Mark kept his position against the dresser until he was sure it was safe. Then he carefully opened the drawer and took out the comic books. The ghoulish face hadn't changed since that afternoon. Its peeling, green skin, bloodshot eyes, and sharp fangs were as hideous as ever. Mark imagined the fright it would've given his mom if she had seen it. Then she would have grounded him for the rest of his life!

As he shoved the comic books into the bottom of his carrying case, he wondered if they were really worth all the fuss. Then he remembered he hadn't read the latest issue of *Tales from the Tomb*.

****

The next morning, Mark's mother gave him last-minute instructions as they drove to Whit's house. He only heard fragments of what she said: "Be polite and respectful, don't talk back, come in when Whit says to, keep your room tidy." His mind was on the adventure that awaited him.

"Are you listening to me?" Julie asked.

Mark looked across the front seat at her. He was sure his blank expression said no. It didn't matter. He knew she knew he wasn't listening. Worse, he knew she knew he knew she knew he wasn't listening. Mothers were born with special radar to scope out daydreaming children.

"I didn't think so," she said with a smile. She put on the turn signal and cruised next to the curb. Mark glanced out the window and found himself staring at a large, Victorian-style house.

"Is this it?" Mark asked, hoping it was.

"Uh huh. Nice, isn't it?"

Mark nodded. In some ways, the house resembled Whit's End; an odd collection of rounded and rectangular shapes all thrown together behind a spacious front porch and large, wooden door. Were there three stories? It was hard to tell, because the roof suddenly jutted upward at strange angles from other parts of the house. The small windows near the top looked like peepholes. He thought of slits he had seen in towers of old castles.

"It's so big," Mark said. "How many rooms do you think it has?"

Julie chuckled and answered, "I don't know. You'll find out before I will."

Mark threw open the car door, grabbed his small case of clothes from the backseat, and walked quickly down the sidewalk to the house. Whit stepped out onto the porch just as Mark climbed the steps.

"Hello there," Whit said warmly. His eyes sparkled beneath bushy, white eyebrows, and he put out his hand.

Mark shook it. "Thanks for letting me stay with you," he said.

"I'm glad to have the company," Whit said, his lips stretching into a wide smile under his thick mustache.

Julie now joined them on the porch, took Whit's hand in hers, and thanked him for taking care of Mark. Whit said it was no trouble at all. He gestured for them to follow him into the house. "Come in. Would you like some tea or coffee?"

"No, thank you," Julie replied. "I'm going to be late for my flight." She turned to Mark and held his face in her hands. "Remember what I told you," she said.

Mark blushed.

"I love you," she said, and then she kissed him.

"Tell Dad I said hello."

She said she would, spun on her heel, and walked briskly back to the car. There was a light spring in her step. Mark couldn't help but think that sometimes she was more like a young girl than a mother.

Whit put his hand on Mark's shoulder, and they both waved. Julie touched the horn in reply. Mark felt a sudden catch in his heart—the kind of feeling he got when he knew he'd be separated from his mom for a while.

"Let's go inside," Whit said.

The house didn't look as big inside as it did from the outside. A small foyer by the front door instantly gave way to a hall, which led to the rest of the first floor. Next to it was a stairway. Whit grabbed Mark's case and escorted him up the stairs to a landing, around a corner to another flight of stairs, and up to the second floor.

The stairwell was lined with frame after frame of photographs—one or two were of a younger-looking Whit, but most were of a woman and three children. Mark assumed Whit wasn't in those because he took the pictures. He wanted to ask who the others were but decided to wait. There was plenty of time for questions later.

Whit put Mark's case in "Jason's room," as he called it. "This is where you'll sleep," he said.

The room was tidy and looked comfortable. A single bed was covered by a multi-colored quilt. Nearby, a nightstand held a lamp with a wood carving of an old sea captain. The captain wore a long coat, sailor's hat, chin beard, and a patch over his right eye. All these were intricately detailed by some woodcrafter's hand. Mark's gaze drifted above the bed to a painting of a ship. Its giant sails billowed in the wind as it cut through foamy waters. Similar paintings and pictures of ancient ships adorned the rest of the walls.

"He liked stories about the sea," Whit explained without being asked. "My son, Jason, I mean. *Moby Dick* was his favorite."

Again Mark had to rethink his image of Whit, not only as a man who was once a husband, but also as a father. He tried to picture Whit sitting in this very room reading bedtime stories to his son.

Along the opposite wall from the bed sat a small desk surrounded by floor-to-ceiling bookshelves. Every inch of the shelves was covered with books.

"Wow!" Mark said. "It's just like the library at Whit's End! Jason must have read a lot."

Whit chuckled and answered, "My wife used to say Jason was the most like me."

"Your wife?" Mark asked.

"Jenny," Whit replied. "She was a wonderful woman. I'll have to tell you about her sometime."

Whit led the way out of Jason's room and pushed open other doors on that floor: a pink and lacy room that had once belonged to his daughter, Jana; a linen closet; the bathroom. Whit's bedroom was at the end of the hall. It was stark in its simplicity. It had a large bed, a dresser, and a tall wardrobe. All were made of the same rich, dark wood. As Mark expected, one wall was covered with shelves full of books.

"That completes our tour of the upstairs," said Whit. "How about downstairs?"

Mark nodded.

As they started down the hall toward the stairs, Mark noticed a door that hadn't been accounted for. *Whit must've forgotten about it,* he thought as he reached for the door handle. "What's this room?" he asked, turning the knob.

"Don't!" Whit snapped.

Mark jumped, backing away from the door.

Whit seemed to realize how harsh he sounded and spoke more gently. "That's just the attic. I don't want you to go up there."

"Oh," said Mark, his heart racing.

Whit looked at Mark and then at the door. "Just the attic," he repeated. He started down the stairs.

Just the attic? Mark wondered. *Then why did Whit snap at me?*

He sneaked a glance back toward the door.

Strange thing, Mark thought. *Especially since the door is locked.*

CHAPTER FOUR

Herald of Hope

Later that morning, Mark met Patti near the gate to the old cemetery. The cloudy sky made the sun look like a flashlight beam shining through a thin blanket.

"Why did you want to meet here?" asked Patti. "You know I don't like this place."

"I thought you wanted to know what was going on," challenged Mark.

"I do!" Patti said.

"Then come on," he said, walking into the graveyard. He wondered if the old man would suddenly appear to scare them as he did the day before. Mark couldn't see anyone.

Except for the squish-squish of their feet on the thick, wet grass, all was silent.

After a moment, Mark said, "After I got to Whit's house this morning, he showed me around."

Patti shivered and said, "You can tell me on the way to town. Let's hurry up and get out of here."

Mark frowned at her but continued. "Whit told me about all his rooms—except one."

Patti looked at him expectantly. "Yeah? Which one?"

"The attic," Mark said. "I was going to open the door, and then he snapped at me."

"He did? Whit doesn't snap at people."

"He did this time. It made me jump."

"But why? I mean, if it's just an attic."

"Because he didn't want me to see what was behind that door."

"It probably had a lot of junk in it," she suggested.

"Oh yeah? Then why was the door *locked?*"

Patti wanted to know what Mark was getting at.

"I don't know," Mark answered quietly. "But it's like . . . he's hiding something."

"Mr. Whittaker? No way. You're making a big deal out of nothing."

Mark shook his head.

"It's those comic books you keep reading!" Patti said.

Mark swung around. "It is not! Why do you keep nagging me about them?"

"Because they're warped, that's why," Patti said sharply. "Ghosts, monsters, dead people . . . they're bad for you."

"What do *you* know?"

"I know your imagination will get out of hand if you read things like that," she replied. "They make you think weird things. I've heard Whit talk about it. We're supposed to fill our minds with good things, he said."

Mark had no defense against a quotation from Whit, and he knew it. "I don't want to talk about it anymore."

By this time, they had reached the grave Whit had visited the day before. It was Jenny Whittaker's grave, just as Patti's parents had said. "Here it is," Mark whispered.

"I still don't understand why you had to see her grave," Patti said.

"Because we didn't see it yesterday," Mark answered. The tombstone was a shiny gray with an ornamental design at the top—a slender angel with a long horn raised to its lips. *Guinevere Renee Whittaker,* "*Jenny,*" *Loving Wife & Mother*, the inscription read. A fresh planter of daffodils stood at the head of the grave. Mark noted that her birthday was February 20 and that she had died on August 17. The daffodils covered the years of her birth and death.

"That's probably why Whit was here," Patti said as she pointed at the second date.

Mark nodded. "It was the anniversary of her death."

"Great. Now let's get out of here," Patti insisted.

"Wait a minute," Mark said. "I just want to—"

"Back again, are you?" growled a low voice behind them. A hand clutched Mark's arm; another grabbed Patti's. It was the old man.

Mark and Patti jumped back with a cry, but the old man held their arms tightly. "Let go!" Mark yelled.

The old man squinted and opened his mouth into a wide, brown-toothed grin that folded his face into creases. "Of course I will, of course I will," he said.

Patti screamed.

"Oh, be quiet," he hissed. "I'll do you no harm. No harm at all."

"Then let us go!" Mark said, straining against the old man's grip.

"It's not often we have kids your age looking around the tombstones," the old man said. "Are you here to pay your respects, or are you playing games?"

"There's no law against looking!" Patti said. Her eyes mirrored both fear and defiance.

"Indeed there isn't, young lady. Indeed there isn't. But as caretaker, I have to know what you're up to. This isn't a relative of yours, is it? You're no relation to Whittaker."

"No. But Mr. Whittaker's a friend of ours," Mark said as he renewed his struggle. "We just wanted to see it!"

"A friend of Whit's, eh?" the old man mused. "Then you'll know all about Jenny Whittaker. All about her."

"We don't know *anything* about her," Patti growled.

"Interesting, it is," the old man said softly. "There are a few things folks don't know."

Once again, that strong feeling of curiosity rose within Mark. "Like what?" he asked.

"Mark!" Patti cried out with disbelief. "He's crazy!"

"The design at the top," the old man said, oblivious to Patti's words. "The angel, you see, with the long horn. Victorian, that is. A design called 'Heralding the Hope.' It's about the hope of the resurrection in Christ."

Mark looked at the design and the angel with the horn lifted upward.

"And if you look just beyond the angel, you'll see a small cloud with a cross in it. Can you see it?" the old man whispered in Mark's ear. His breath smelled of licorice.

Mark squinted to see the small cloud, hardly aware that the old man's grip had slackened and his hand had fallen away.

Patti noticed instantly and started to run. She slipped on the wet grass with a loud splat, scrambled to her feet, and finally stopped at a safe distance. "Mark!" she called.

But Mark was fascinated by the tombstone. He took a step forward to get a closer look at the angel, the trumpet, and the delicate cloud.

"Mark!" Patti shouted again.

To his amazement, Mark could see a cross, nearly hidden by the billowy clouds so artistically carved.

"Nobody ever notices it," the old man said forlornly as he pulled a wooden pipe from his ragged coat pocket.

"Something so pretty, and nobody stops to look. You kids certainly wouldn't take the time. Never do."

"Mark!" Patti shouted again, edging closer.

"Wow," Mark said. He reached out and touched the cold stone. It sent a startling chill through him, and he jerked back. Suddenly he realized he was standing on top of the grave. "Oh no!" he gasped, leaping to one side.

Patti waved frantically. "Come on, Mark! What's the matter with you?"

"I stepped on her grave!" he called out apologetically.

The old man clamped the pipe in his teeth and said, "You're not telling me you're superstitious, now are you? Walking on the dead—is that what you think you're doing?"

Mark's face went crimson. "I've heard that it's disrespectful, that's all," he said.

"Maybe it would be disrespectful if she was buried here," the old man said, producing a lit match like a magician who pulls a rabbit out of a hat. "But she's not."

Mark's mouth fell open. "What?"

The old man cleared his throat and placed the lit match against the pipe. "That's the other thing most folks don't know. Jenny Whittaker isn't buried here. This is a memorial."

Mark glanced anxiously at Patti, who now stood even closer.

"Then . . . where is she?" Mark gulped.

"Ah, but that's the question, isn't it?" the old man replied, scratching his cheek. "That's the question."

Mark looked at the tombstone again. The herald of hope. He stared at the name on the tombstone and found himself thinking of the locked door.

CHAPTER FIVE

Jenny's Fight

*I*f *Jenny Whittaker isn't buried in her grave, then where is she?* Mark wondered. Once Patti got over her scare at the cemetery and her anger at Mark for making her go there, she agreed to help him solve the mystery.

"How do we know the old man was telling the truth?" Patti challenged Mark as they watched a softball game at McCalister Park.

"Why would he lie to us?"

"Because he's a weird old man who likes to scare kids, that's why."

Mark shook his head. "I don't think so. Didn't you hear

35

the way he talked about the herald of hope or whatever it was called? He's the caretaker of the cemetery—next to a *church*. He wouldn't lie to us."

"Yeah, but he wouldn't tell you anything else about it, either," Patti countered.

Later, Mark and Patti went to a pond near Tom Riley's farm, where Mark swam and Patti lounged on the bank because of her cast. She dangled her toes in the water and asked why anyone would go to the trouble to have a grave but not put a body in it.

Mark floated on his back and considered the question. "The old man said it was a memorial. People put up plaques and monuments without putting dead bodies underneath them, right?"

"I guess so," Patti said, then absentmindedly kicked water at Mark.

"So, where's her body?" Mark asked. "Why wouldn't Whit bury his wife in Odyssey?"

Patti leaned back and sighed. "Maybe she didn't like it here."

At Whit's End, their last stop of the afternoon, Mark and Patti watched Whit as he worked behind the ice cream counter. He laughed and joked with his young customers who had come from all over town to enjoy the food and fun of this discovery emporium.

Mark looked puzzled. "Where *did* he bury her, Patti?"

"I don't know, Mark. Why don't you ask him? He's right over there."

Mark grimaced.

"He's our friend, right?" she insisted. "He'll tell us. I feel like we're being sneaky, talking about him and making wild guesses about his wife. Let's ask him."

Mark rejected the idea. "Right. What would we say? 'Uh, excuse me, Whit, but could you tell us where your wife is buried?'"

"Well, it's better than all this creepy guessing. We're talking about a *body*. It gives me the chills," Patti said. "Besides, she could be buried anywhere."

"Or nowhere at all," Mark said thoughtfully.

"What?"

"Maybe she isn't buried," Mark said.

Patti's eyes widened and then narrowed as they always did when she got mad at him. She shook her finger at him, and Mark knew what she was going to say. *It's those comic books. They're warping your mind. Now you're thinking sick things about Mr. Whittaker's wife, and it's wrong.*

But Patti didn't say a word. She simply growled and turned away.

****

That evening, Whit prepared some barbecued chicken, potatoes, and assorted vegetables for dinner. He and Mark sat down, and, after praying, they began to chat about the

day as they ate their food. Whit explained that he was working on a new idea for the Imagination Station. He hoped to
have it working well enough to bring it up from his workroom in the basement of Whit's End so all the kids could use
it.

"What's wrong? Don't you like your chicken?" Whit
suddenly asked.

Mark was surprised by the question until he realized he
had just been picking at his food. "No, it's good," Mark said.
He took a bite of the chicken just to prove it.

Whit cocked an eyebrow and said, "There's something
on your mind."

"No, sir," Mark said after he swallowed his food.

"Are you sure?" Whit persisted.

It occurred to Mark that this might be the only chance
he'd have to talk about Jenny, so he worked up his courage
and did just that. "Patti and I took a shortcut through the
cemetery yesterday, and . . . we saw you," he said softly.

"Oh?"

"You were putting flowers on your wife's grave."

"That's right," Whit said. "It was the anniversary of her
death. Why didn't you say something sooner?"

Mark shrugged and said, "I don't know. I figured it was . . .
you know."

"Hard for me to talk about?"

"Yeah," Mark said.

Whit reached over and touched Mark's arm. "Mark, I've

always said that you should never be afraid to ask me about anything—and I meant it."

Mark looked at Whit sheepishly, suddenly embarrassed for making such a big deal out of nothing. "Will you tell me about her?"

Whit sat back in his chair, rubbed his mouth with his napkin, and then tossed it onto the table. "All right, I'll tell you."

Whit explained that he had met Jenny in Pasadena, California, when he was a student in college there. She worked in the library. At first, they didn't like each other much. They argued about books and philosophies and ideas, until one day they realized that something special was happening between them. They were becoming friends. In time, friendship led to a deeper relationship. Whit finally asked her out on a date, and a short time later they married.

"How did she die?" Mark asked abruptly, bypassing years of Whit and Jenny's life together.

Whit stroked his mustache and looked at Mark thoughtfully. "That's a more complicated story. Are you sure you want to hear about it?"

Mark assured Whit that he did.

"Well, Jenny's death and the creation of Whit's End are tied together. Did you know that?"

Mark shook his head no.

Whit began, "There was a building called the Fillmore Recreation Center. It used to be a meeting place for all kinds of activities for the townspeople. But they built a new center in the middle of McCalister Park and left the old one to rot. It was falling apart, and some of the folks in Odyssey thought it should be torn down and replaced with a shopping center. My wife had other ideas. She was the leader of a movement to have the building restored and turned into a cultural landmark."

Mark asked what he meant by "cultural landmark."

"Have you heard how some cities have buildings that are real old and people turn them into museums or give tours of them? That's what Jenny wanted the Fillmore Building to become."

"I get it," Mark said.

"Anyway, Jenny worked hard to save the building," Whit continued. "But not everyone in town agreed with her. In fact, *I* was one of them. I couldn't figure out why she was wearing herself down fighting for such a wreck of a building." Whit paused for a moment and chuckled at something he remembered. "Boy, we had some red-hot debates about it, you can be sure. I think she was just using me for practice before tackling the city council. She was very outspoken in those meetings. She was a determined woman."

"You mean she gave speeches and stuff like that?" Mark asked.

Whit nodded. "Uh huh. All over town. She was desperate to win support. The town argued about it for months, but she never gave up. Then, at the town meeting when the city council was going to make its final decision, she collapsed suddenly."

"What happened?"

Whit was quiet for a moment, and Mark wasn't sure he'd answer. Finally he said, "At first I thought she was simply exhausted. She worked so hard, but . . . it was far more serious than that. She had a disease in her kidney that had poisoned her entire body. The doctors couldn't do anything for her and . . . she died that same day."

Again there was a long silence. Mark looked away, afraid that Whit might start to cry or something.

"I was crushed by losing her," Whit eventually said. "I felt bitter, too. I blamed Odyssey for her death. I locked myself away."

Mark glanced back at Whit and was relieved to see he was dry-eyed. "What happened then?"

"A month or so went by, and I was visited by Tom Riley, my best friend. You know Tom."

Mark did. Tom Riley had once shot Mark in the rear end with a water pistol for picking apples from his tree.

Whit continued, "Tom was a member of the city council. He said that because of Jenny's death, the decision about the Fillmore Building hadn't been made, but that it would be the next day. He persuaded me that Jenny's fight for the Fillmore Building wasn't a waste of time, that she often spoke of its potential as a place for kids to play and learn. He said he thought it would be a shame to lose the battle now.

"The building was doomed and the gavel was just about to fall when I burst into the room and said I'd buy the Fillmore myself." He chuckled as he added, "I've always had a weak spot for dramatic entrances."

"So the Fillmore Building became Whit's End?" Mark asked.

"Yep," Whit said with a smile. "A place of adventure and discovery where kids of all ages can just be kids. All because of Jenny."

A flash of heat lightning made Mark realize the sun was nearly gone. They had been talking for almost two hours.

Whit grabbed the dinner dishes and took them to the sink. "That's enough about me. How about a game of checkers?"

****

They laughed as they played checkers, particularly when they began to make up the rules as they went along. Then they played a game Whit had created to test the players' memories. The game turned the entire living room into a giant board game, with Whit and Mark as living, moving pieces. Finally, they found some man-sized cardboard boxes and turned them into "time-traveling" submarines. They decided to call it a night after Whit accidentally torpedoed an end table and broke a lamp.

When it was time for bed, Whit remembered that he wanted to give Mark a spare housekey so he could get in and out during the day. "Come on. It's up in my room," Whit said as he turned off all the downstairs lights.

Mark watched as Whit fished through some keys he kept in a commemorative cup on top of his dresser. It struck Mark that the key to the attic might be in that cup, too.

"Here it is!" Whit announced, handing a key to Mark. Mark glanced at it, then shoved it into his pocket and said good night.

A few minutes later, while brushing his teeth in the bathroom, Mark realized he hadn't found out from Whit where Jenny was buried. Even though Whit had said he'd answer any of Mark's questions, Mark couldn't bring himself to ask. In the back of his mind, he knew Whit would think he was warped to even think of such a thing.

Mark went back to his room and gently closed the door. As he pulled pajamas out of his carrying case, his fingers brushed against his comic books. *Tales of Horror and Mystery* was on top. He tossed it onto the bed and pondered the cover as he slipped into his night clothes. "Shadows in the Night," shouted the headline. Under the headline, a stern-looking woman holding a candle climbed a dark stairway. Behind her, a menacing shadow with outstretched arms reached toward her.

Mark climbed into bed, opened to the first page, and stopped. It was the story of a man who returned from the dead to seek revenge on his wicked wife.

What would Whit think about this? Mark wondered as the

moss-covered man—no longer just a shadow—made his appearance during his wife's dinner party. *Would he approve or disapprove?*

Probably disapprove, Mark thought. He sighed and dropped the comic book next to the bed. He couldn't shake the image of Jenny Whittaker's empty grave and the locked door to the attic.

Another flash of heat lightning lit up the night. Mark shuddered. *Maybe Patti's right*, he ventured. His imagination *was* out of control. He grabbed the comic book and shoved it into his case.

He turned off the light on the sea-captain lamp and fell quickly into a deep sleep.

****

Thump.

The noise woke Mark up.

Someone just closed my door, he thought. He rolled over to look. For a moment, he thought it was his mom checking in on him. Then he remembered it couldn't be his mom because she was in Washington, D.C. This wasn't his home or his own bed. He was at Whit's house. In Jason's room.

He sleepily rubbed his eyes and tried to focus them. The only light came from under the door. Somebody was in the hall. He saw the shadow of moving feet. *A shadow*, he thought, and his mind raced to the moss-covered man in the comic book.

He clutched the covers and looked around. Was something in the room with him?

The digital display on the clock across the room blazed at him with red eyes: *12:15.*

Thump.

The shadow beneath the door disappeared. Mark could hear gentle footsteps pad down the hall, then stop. There was a rattling sound, then a familiar click. *That's the sound of a key in a lock,* Mark thought. Then he heard the rasp of a latch and the turn of a doorknob as the door slid open on creaking hinges. The footsteps tapped up a flight of stairs until they faded into silence.

The attic, Mark thought. *Whit's gone up into the attic.*

He rolled onto his back and swallowed hard with a spitless throat. It was like one of the stories he read in the *Fright Frenzy* comic book about a mad, wooden-legged pirate who haunted an inn looking for his dead shipmates. The tap, tap, tap of his wooden leg would echo through the hallways as the guests tried to sleep. Years later, historians found skeletons trapped behind a brick wall in a secret room of the inn.

What in the world is up in that attic?

In the dark room, his mind turned to even darker thoughts.

CHAPTER SIX

The Embarrassing Truth

"A mad pirate . . . brick walls . . . shadows . . . " Patti mumbled and rubbed her cast as if she had an itch. Her eyes were fixed straight ahead, almost as if she were in shock. Mark chewed the inside of his lip. They were sitting on a bench in McCalister Park.

While he waited for Patti's response, Mark watched kids go in and out the front door to Whit's End. One boy waved to Mark before he disappeared inside. Mark halfheartedly waved back. The movement of his hand broke Patti's spell.

"You're crazy," she said, turning to face him without blinking. "You've lost all your marbles."

"I knew you'd say that," Mark said with a frown.

"What else am I supposed to say? You're trying to tell me that Mr. Whittaker is keeping *his wife* in the attic, and you think I'm going to agree with you?"

Mark spread his arms defensively. "Why not? Isn't that what happened in Sleeping Beauty?"

"That's a fairy tale!"

"And I read that the Russians keep the body of Lenin in a glass coffin. It's kind of a memorial. Isn't that what the old man said—Jenny was in a memorial?"

Patti looked disgusted. "Her *grave* is a memorial!"

"Yeah, but—"

"It's sick and *you're* sick, and I'm going to tell your mother about your scary comic books because they have *warped your brain!*"

Mark leaped to his feet and paced in front of her. "Will you quit badgering me about those comic books? I heard him sneak up the stairs to the attic in the middle of the night. Why would he do that? What else could he have up there?"

"Old books, model airplanes—how should I know? But it never occurred to me that he might—" She stopped as if choking on the words. "I don't even want to say it. You're sick."

"I am not," Mark said. "And you better not say anything to my mom about those comic books."

Patti sneered at him, "I won't have to say anything. You're acting so weird that she'll figure it out for herself."

"Look, Patti—"

"Look *nothing*, Mark! You're getting really weird about this, and I don't want anything to do with it. Understand?" She folded her arms as if they would somehow lock out any further discussion.

"Then what am I supposed to do?" Mark pleaded. "How am I going to find out the truth?"

"Why don't you ask the old man in the cemetery since you're such good pals with him now," she mocked.

Mark kicked a stone angrily and looked in the direction of the church. Its tower rose high above the trees of McCalister Park.

****

Mark was certain the old man would see him and suddenly appear from behind a tree or a tombstone. But he didn't. So Mark stood in front of the church and debated with himself about whether to go inside. He decided to circle around first, just in case the old man was outside working. He felt safer talking in the light of day anyway. A dark church seemed too spooky to Mark, considering his present frame of mind.

"Hello?" Mark called out. "Mr. Caretaker?"

A large blackbird squawked at him. Mark jumped, then continued on. Eventually, he heard the scraping sound of a spade in dirt. *He's digging a grave*, Mark thought with a tremble. He stopped where he was and had another debate with himself. Did he really want to know about Whit's wife *this badly?*

Yes, he thought. *It's just an old man shoveling dirt, that's all. Nothing to worry about, nothing to fear.* He forced himself to go on.

Near the rear of the church, Mark could see the top of the old man's head. Then he heard grunting and more digging and saw an occasional shower of dirt as the shovel was hoisted above the hole.

Mark approached cautiously and peered down. The old man was wearing the same ragged clothes he had worn the day before. The wooden pipe jutted out of thin, compressed lips that were hardly distinguishable from the other lines on his face.

The old man looked at Mark and said, "What do you want now?"

"I just, uh, wanted to, uh—" Mark stammered, then composed himself. "Are you digging a *grave?*"

"Maybe my own if I don't find that leaky water pipe soon," he snorted. "The basement's flooded."

"Oh," Mark said, a little disappointed. Digging a grave was far more exciting than digging for broken water pipes.

The old man wiped his brow with a dirty handkerchief. "I know why you're here," he said.

"You do?"

"I do, I do," he cackled, then coughed harshly. "Your mind's been working hard since you were here yesterday, hasn't it?"

Mark blushed. "Well . . ."

"Got the whiff of a mystery, didn't you?" The old man

poked the shovel into the ground, rested his elbow on it, and fished in his pocket for a moment. He found some matches and relighted his pipe. "A real mystery."

Mark felt annoyed as he suddenly realized the old man was playing some sort of game with him. "Are you teasing me?"

"What do you think?" The old man laughed and coughed.

"You said Jenny Whittaker wasn't buried here," Mark complained.

"Well, she isn't," he said. "You think I lied to you? A liar, am I?"

"No, sir," Mark answered more quietly.

"You kids think you know it all, don't you? Well, you don't," he grumbled.

"Yes, sir."

The old man chuckled again. "Couldn't work up the nerve to ask Whit, could you?" he asked.

Mark wondered how the old man knew so much. Was this a game he played with other kids who happened through the graveyard? "No," Mark replied.

"Nope. Knew you wouldn't," the old man said proudly. "Even Whit can't get the kids to talk to him about *everything*."

Mark resented that the old man spoke with such pride— as if he had accomplished some small victory for himself. "Where is Whit's wife?" Mark asked directly.

The old man shook his head. "Not here, that's for sure. Nope. She's not buried in Odyssey at all."

"Then where is she? Please tell me."

"I should make you guess, but I've got work to do." The old man mopped his brow again. "She's in Callee-forn-eye-a."

"What?"

"California!" the old man snapped.

Mark stared at him as if he didn't understand.

"Pasadena, California. Whit had her put in her family's mausoleum in Pasadena, California," he said as he picked up the shovel.

"A mausoleum?" Mark wondered aloud.

The old man looked at Mark impatiently. "Are you deaf? I said a *mausoleum*. A crypt. A vault in the middle of a cemetery. Rich folks use them to bury their dead, you know—stone houses for their mortal remains."

"She's buried in California?" Mark asked numbly.

"Where'd you think she was—Whit's basement?" the old man growled. Then he returned to his digging.

Not exactly, Mark wanted to say. Instead he asked, "Why didn't you tell me yesterday?"

"That woulda been too easy. Too easy by a mile. I thought I'd give you something to chew on. I know how you kids are. Get bored in the summertime and you get in trouble. Take to wandering around my cemetery. Bet you like ghost stories, don't you?"

Mark turned and walked away. He felt as if a cruel trick had been played on him.

"You wanna hear about ol' George McCalister's grave?"

the old man said with a laugh and a cough. "There's a story that'll keep you awake nights!"

****

Mark found an empty corner booth in Whit's End where he thought he could brood in peace. Across the room, Patti stood at the center of a small group of kids. One was signing her cast.

Mark looked away. At the moment, he didn't care much for Patti. She had lectured him for ten minutes after he told her what the old man said. She called him twisted and mean and a disloyal friend to Whit. He thought she was being extremely cold-hearted, considering how ashamed and embarrassed he already felt for thinking such morbid things about Whit's wife.

They stood in stony silence in front of Whit's End for a few minutes, each waiting for the other to apologize. Neither one would. Then, when she said she wanted to go into Whit's End to get people to sign her cast, he angrily said she was just using it to get attention. She called him a creep, he called her conceited, and they stormed into Whit's End and went their separate ways.

Mark knew he should apologize. The argument was his fault. But he had suffered enough humiliation for one day and couldn't bring himself to do it. So he was wrong about Jenny Whittaker. That still didn't explain why Whit was being so mysterious about the attic—why he locked the door. And, for the first time, it struck him that he had only a few more days to sort it all out.

He lowered his head, tore a napkin into little pieces, and tried to come up with a plan.

"Making a nest?" Whit asked as he slid behind the opposite side of the table.

Mark jerked his head up. Shame and embarrassment washed over him anew.

Whit pointed to the scraps of napkin now collected on the table. "A nest," he repeated with a smile.

Mark shook his head and glanced away. Patti had found someone else to sign her cast. But her eyes were on Mark. She watched with interest now that Whit was with him.

"Is something wrong?" asked Whit.

Mark considered coming right out and asking Whit about the attic. It would be the smart thing to do, he figured. Whit was his friend. He would be honest about it. And if it wasn't any of Mark's business, Whit would say that, too. Wasn't that how friendship was supposed to work? Maybe so. But maybe the old man was right. There were some things he couldn't say, even to Whit.

"I had a fight with Patti," Mark finally offered.

"I guessed," Whit responded. "What was it about?"

Mark thought carefully, scrambling for an answer other than the truth. "She . . . she blames me because her arm's in a cast."

"Does she?"

"Yeah. And I know she's over there right now telling everybody how it happened and how it's my fault."

"I don't think she'd do that," Whit said. "Besides, it wasn't really your fault, was it?"

"Sort of," he replied. "Even when she doesn't say it, I know that's what she's thinking."

"You're a mind reader now?" Whit said with a chuckle.

Mark shrugged.

Whit burrowed into the napkin remains with his finger and said tenderly, "I wouldn't pretend to know how Patti feels about you or the things that led to her breaking her arm. You'll have to talk to her about that. But you knew it would take a while for her to trust you again."

"Yeah, I know," Mark said softly. This wasn't what he wanted to talk about, yet he felt glad that they were.

"It's possible that the cast makes you feel guilty about what happened—even if she doesn't say so out loud," Whit observed. "People often have a hard time letting old wounds heal. Sometimes it's even harder when you have something that serves as a reminder. Like a cast."

Mark's expression betrayed his confusion.

"I didn't realize my pearls of wisdom were so hard to understand. I'll have to work on that," Whit said with a laugh. "All I'm saying is, let it go. Don't let her cast bother you. And don't assume she's thinking something that she's not."

Mark looked across the room again. Patti was still watching them. Though he wasn't a mind reader, at that moment

Mark was sure he knew what she was thinking. She was thinking he should ask Whit about the attic. *I should,* he thought. The old man didn't have to be right.

He opened his mouth to do it. He even silently formed the words. But he couldn't ask. He would look for another chance to ask—or another way to find out. Not now. Later. There was still time.

Whit slid out from the table and stood up. "There's something else I need to tell you," he said.

Mark looked up at Whit's round and friendly face.

"Your mother called this afternoon. She wanted to talk to you. I guess she thought you'd be here."

Mark searched Whit's face expectantly. *More news,* he thought. *They decided to get back together.* His stomach tightened.

"We've arranged a flight for you," Whit said.

"A flight?"

"Your parents want you to join them in Washington for a few days," he said with a big grin.

Mark's heart began to pound. "They want me to fly to Washington? Why?"

Whit shrugged and replied, "I suppose they want you to be with them. She didn't say. I'm sorry."

That didn't dampen Mark's excitement. "When do I go?" he asked.

"Tomorrow."

CHAPTER SEVEN

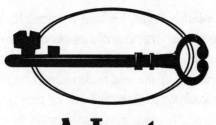

A Last Chance

Mark left Whit and Patti at Whit's End. His excuse was that he needed to go back to Whit's house to pack for the flight. The real reason was that he felt mixed up about leaving and was afraid he might blurt out everything about the attic, Jenny's grave, and his suspicions.

How could he feel happy and sad at the same time? He was happy because he would fly to Washington to be with his parents. He was sad because now he would never find out what was in Whit's attic.

He should've asked Whit directly, he knew. But he realized how stupid it would sound. Real stupid.

Patti's probably right, he said to himself. *There's probably nothing in that attic but old books or model planes or a stamp collection. Why make a big deal about it? I should curb my curiosity. If the old man wanted to give me something to think about to keep me out of trouble, he gave me the wrong thing. In fact, my whole brain is filled with the wrong things.*

As he reached for the handle to Whit's front door, Mark made a vow to himself. He promised to throw away all the comic books. "And," he continued out loud, "it doesn't matter what's in the attic!" He pushed open the door, never suspecting the temptation that awaited him.

The sky rumbled ominously. It began to rain again.

****

Large raindrops lashed at the window in Jason's room where Mark packed his case. The fading light bled through the pane and swirled like haunted shadows on the bedspread.

Mark shoved another shirt into his case and felt the comic books at the bottom. He considered throwing them away right then, but he didn't want Whit to find them later. He'd wait until he could find a large outdoor trash can.

The phone rang. Mark stepped into the hallway, unsure of where the phone was. He followed the sound into Whit's bedroom and found it on the nightstand next to the bed. He picked up the receiver and said sheepishly, "Hello, John Whittaker's residence."

"Hello, Mark," Whit said above the din of Whit's End. "I'm glad I found you."

"Was I lost?" Mark asked innocently.

Whit laughed heartily. "I meant—oh, never mind. I'm really sorry about this, but I got a call from Tom Riley, and there's a zoning meeting I have to attend at City Hall tonight. Do you mind?"

"It's okay," Mark answered as he turned and casually scanned the room.

"There's a plate of food in the refrigerator for you. Just warm it up in the microwave. Three minutes should do the trick. All right? I won't be very late."

Mark's gaze fell on Whit's dresser and the cup full of keys. "Okay, thanks," he said.

"Bye-bye."

"Bye," Mark said and hung up the phone. *Keys,* he thought. *Whit won't be home for a while. The attic.* He walked around the bed to the dresser and, for a moment, argued with himself. *Don't touch the keys,* his conscience said. But that strong feeling of curiosity rose up once more to remind him this was his only chance to find out what was in the attic.

By the time he reached the cup, he knew he couldn't turn back. It was too perfect. He would find the key, go up to the attic, satisfy his curiosity, and come back down. No one would ever know.

Still, his heart hammered against his chest as he picked up the cup and began to search for a key to the attic door. He had no idea what it should look like. There were copper, gold, and silver keys; round, rectangular, and square keys. Mark figured it would take half an hour just to try them all in the lock.

His eye caught a long, slender key with a hollow circle on one end and a simple cut of teeth on the other. A "skeleton key," he remembered his grandmother calling this kind. They had one or two stuck in closet doors back at his house. He decided to try it first.

His hands trembled as he approached the attic door and aimed the key at the lock. Maybe Whit would suddenly appear behind him. Or an alarm would go off. Or someone would scream at him maniacally from the other side of the door.

He hesitated, took a deep breath, and then slid the key into the lock.

Ring!

Mark nearly leaped out of his skin, sure that he had been caught.

Ring! the sound came again.

He leaned weakly against the wall as he realized with great relief that it was the phone. *The phone!*

He raced to answer it, his mind ablaze with apologies and excuses in case it was Whit and he somehow knew what Mark was up to.

It was Patti.

"Hi, Mark," she said.

"Hi, Patti," he said curtly.

"I heard you were leaving tomorrow and, well, I thought

it might be a couple of weeks before I see you again because I might be at camp by the time you get back and, you know, I was thinking about . . ."

Mark held the phone away and tapped his foot impatiently. Didn't she realize he was busy? He pressed the phone against his ear again. Too late, he realized she was apologizing.

". . . it was all really silly and, well, I hope we can still be friends and forget about the whole thing, because I'd hate it if you left and we were still mad at each other."

"Yeah, okay," Mark said quickly. *Whit could come home any minute!* he thought, chewing the inside of his lip.

"Yeah, okay," Patti said. She seemed surprised that making up could happen so quickly. "So . . . I guess you're sorry, too."

"Uh huh," Mark said. "I'll see you when I get back."

"What?"

"I said I'll see you when I get back."

Patti's tone went hard. "You want to get off the phone, don't you?"

"Well, uh—"

"Mark Prescott, you are one of the rudest boys I've ever known in my life!" Patti hung up with a loud click.

Mark listened to the buzz of the receiver. For a second, he thought he should call her back and apologize. But only for a second. He dashed back to the attic door, where the key still waited for his attention. He held his breath, turned the key, and heard the lock click! As he clasped the doorknob, it was cold to his touch. Every muscle in his body tightened involuntarily. He looked down at his hand on the knob and felt as if it belonged to someone else—in a picture, maybe.

Do you realize what you're about to do? his conscience asked. *You're about to go into a forbidden room.*

That's right, Mark replied. *But I'll only be in there a minute—just long enough to see what's there. Then I'll come out and never think about it again. I promise.*

Mark didn't give his conscience another chance to argue. He opened the door and walked into the dark passageway.

CHAPTER EIGHT

The Top of the Stairs

At the base of the stairs, Mark fumbled for a light switch, found it, and flipped it on. A dim light shone at the top of the stairs. Mark pondered the yellow glow and the ten wooden stairs he had to climb to see what waited for him. With lead feet, he took the first step. A musty smell drifted down and got sucked past him by the fresh air in the hallway. He took another step. Then another.

It hadn't occurred to him that he might be putting himself in serious danger. Not until now.

But it's Whit's house, he reasoned as he slowed his pace.

Yeah, sure, his conscience suddenly spoke again. *Just*

like you reasoned that Jenny Whittaker might be up here.

Mark shivered as his skin went goose-pimply. Although Mrs. Whittaker was safely buried in Pasadena, California, Mark couldn't easily shake off the notion that she might be in the attic.

Nah. It's just a cold attic, he assured himself as he rubbed his arms. But he knew it was a lie. The attic air was thick and warm from the summer heat.

Frightening images from his collection of comic books paraded before him. Closets of skeletons, basements of madmen, attics of . . . *of what?*

He stopped to consider his options. What if something hideous suddenly lunged at him? What if he saw something so terrible that he would never have a decent night's sleep again? What if Whit's secret was so disgusting that he could never go back to Whit's End or look Whit in the eye?

He listened carefully. Secretly, he hoped the slightest sound would give him an excuse to run away. But he heard nothing except the thumping of his heart and the occasional creak of the steps beneath his feet.

This bolstered his courage enough to climb a couple more stairs. He was now eye level with the attic floor. He pushed up on his feet and peered cautiously over the wooden planks. To his surprise, it looked like most attics. Wooden beams stretched up to the peak of the A-frame. The mustiness was stronger and carried with it years of pink insulation, scattered junk, cardboard boxes, unused clothes, outdated appliances, and yellow paper—spread throughout in various clusters with no apparent order.

Just an attic, Mark thought, disappointed.

He climbed the rest of the stairs and stood confidently in this room that had consumed him for the past few days.

Just an attic, he thought again.

Then he saw it. A section in a far corner was set up as a room. It was furnished with an immaculately made bed, shelves full of books, high school pennants tacked to the wall, a small student's desk and study lamp—all carefully placed on a large, antique rug. It was a well-ordered island in a sea of clutter.

Wide-eyed, Mark walked to the room and browsed like a patron in a museum. That, in fact, is what it reminded Mark of: a museum. Except this one had a small layer of dust all over it.

The pennants on the wall, the "high adventure" books on the shelves, and the sports trophies lining a small dresser were dead giveaways. It was a boy's room. But it was a boy's room from another time. Mark had seen rooms like it on television shows from the late 1950s and 1960s.

He spied three framed photographs on a shelf. One was a black and white of a freckled, light-haired boy playing happily in a sandbox. The other, also black and white, was of the same boy—older now—with a dark-haired, mustache-free Whit proudly holding up a large fish.

Who is this kid? Mark wondered.

He looked at the third photo. It was in color but faded, and it showed the boy—a teen now—wearing a Santa Claus hat and hugging a dark-haired, mustachioed Whit in front of a brilliantly decorated Christmas tree.

Mark felt that catch in his heart again—the same one he felt when his mother left.

His eye caught a yellowing newspaper clipping on the small student's desk. "Jerry Whittaker Killed in Action," the headline shouted. The article had a photograph of a more-adult version of the light-haired boy. He was wearing a uniform. Behind him was the American flag.

Jerry Whittaker.

He looked closer. The article explained that Jerry Whittaker, son of John and Jenny Whittaker, was killed in a skirmish in Vietnam. *Killed in a skirmish.*

Mark's head spun with the news, and he suddenly remembered the photos on the wall of the second-floor stairwell. They pictured Whit, Jenny, and *three* kids. But Whit spoke only of Jason and Jana. *Why?* he wondered.

Mark picked up a paperweight fashioned from red clay to look like an Indian head. It was obviously handmade and crudely done. His fingers felt ridges on the bottom, so he turned it over. There, in youthful script, it said: "To Dad, with all my love, Jerry." Mark closed his eyes and pictured it. Whit came up to this room and sat at this desk to read the article, hold this handmade gift, and drift into memories. Mark understood. He sometimes did the same thing in his own room after his mother and father split up. He would hold the baseball glove his dad bought him and let his mind sail to better times.

Mark wondered if Whit cried the way he sometimes did. He looked again at the article. Near the bottom, the ink sprayed out in several circles. Fallen tears.

Bang! A door slammed like a gunshot.

Mark gasped and dropped the paperweight. It broke into three pieces with a dull crack.

"Mark?" came Whit's muffled voice from far below.

Oh no oh no oh no oh no oh no, Mark's soul cried.

Panicked, he grabbed up the three pieces and, glancing around quickly to see where to hide them, decided to shove them into the back of a desk drawer. He dashed on tiptoes across the attic to the stairs, then down to the hallway, bracing himself for Whit's appearance.

"Mark!" Whit called again.

He's in the kitchen was Mark's frenzied guess as he closed the attic door as quietly as possible. He wasted precious moments searching in his pockets for the key, only to realize it was still in the lock.

"Anybody here?" Whit called again, this time from the front hall. He was making his way to the stairs.

Mark couldn't get the latch to turn. *Oh no oh no oh no oh no oh no*. His silent moan was fast becoming a shrill scream in his head. Whit was in the foyer now, and Mark pushed on the attic door. The latch clicked.

"Mark," Whit called from the bottom of the stairs. Just around the corner. So much closer now.

Mark searched the hall for an escape. Instantly he knew that if he tried to get to his room, Whit would see him from the landing and suspect something. Instead, Mark turned in the opposite direction and ran into the bathroom. He quietly closed the door, waited a few seconds, then flushed the toilet. *Whit will think I've been in here the whole time and couldn't hear him*, Mark hoped.

Turning the faucet on, he shoved his hands under the cold water. *This will make it look authentic*, he thought. He dried his hands and turned to the door. Bracing himself for whatever might happen next, he opened the bathroom door and stepped back into the hall. Whit stood at the top of the stairs.

"There you are," Whit said with a smile.

CHAPTER NINE

In Hot Water

"**A**re you sick?" Whit asked.

"No," Mark answered, surprised by the question.

"You look pale," Whit said.

Mark rubbed his face self-consciously. "What happened to your meeting?" he said. "I thought you'd be home later."

"Cancelled," said Whit. He frowned and stepped closer to Mark. "Are you sure you're all right? You look like something's wrong."

"I do?" Mark touched his face and wished he had checked himself in the bathroom mirror.

Whit reached over and pressed his hand against Mark's

69

forehead. "You don't feel like you have a temperature. What were you doing?"

"I was just getting ready to leave tomorrow," stammered Mark.

"Ah, yes," said Whit. "You're leaving in the morning. Are you all packed?"

"Uh huh."

Whit stroked his mustache thoughtfully. "Well, I may as well say it now. I'll be sad to see you go."

"Really?"

"Of course! You've always been good company, Mark."

Mark didn't know what to say.

Whit winked at him, then rubbed his hands together. "I think you should have a bath so you'll be clean for the flight in the morning. Then we'll see what kind of trouble we can get into."

"Trouble?" Mark squeaked.

Whit chuckled. "Fun, Mark. Are you absolutely sure you're all right?"

"Yeah," Mark said.

Whit stepped past him into the bathroom and ran the water. It roared in the hollow of the tub—an old-fashioned, snow-white type that was long and sloped and sat on stubby feet. "There you go," Whit said as he walked out of the bathroom. "Just shout if you need anything."

Mark closed the door and began to undress. His heart was still beating fast. *What am I gonna do? Whit'll find that Indian head sooner or later, and he'll know I broke it!*

He dropped his clothes on the floor as an agonizing thought struck him. *What an idiot I am! I should've left the Indian head on the floor! Whit would assume it fell off on its own or something. Tucked in that drawer, he'll know someone put it there on purpose.*

Mark stepped into the tub. It was a little too hot, so he adjusted the faucet handles accordingly. The continual roar of the water was soothing. It was as if the sound protected him, hid him. He leaned back, stretched out, and let the water cover him.

How am I gonna tell Whit? Mark asked himself over and over. He knew he would have to. There was no returning to the attic to disguise what he'd done, no chance to fix it before Whit discovered it.

He tried to picture himself breaking the news to Whit. *I'm sorry, Mr. Whittaker, but I stole your key, snuck up into the attic after you told me not to, and, while I was there, broke your prized Indian head that your dead son made for you when he was little.*

Oh, brother.

He let himself soak for a long time before applying any soap. *Maybe I can leave for Washington and he won't go up there for a long time. When he finally does, he'll forget I was here and think he broke it himself and . . .*

No way.

After giving himself a thorough wash, Mark climbed out of the tub, pulled the plug by the beaded chain, and dried off. *Maybe Mom and Dad really will get back together again, and we'll stay at our home in Washington, and I'll never have to face Whit or explain what happened.* Mark shook the thought away.

As he stooped to pick up his clothes, he noticed the old-fashioned key in the bathroom door lock. *It looks just like the attic door key*, he thought.

Then he put his hand over his mouth in horror as he realized, *The attic door key! I didn't put it back in the cup!*

Mark tossed his towel aside and snatched up his clothes. He checked the pockets and the folds and shook them in hopes that he would find the key. Not once, not twice, but three times, just to be sure. Then he searched around the bathroom—the tub, the sink, the bathmat, and every inch of the tiled floor. Nothing.

Oh no oh no oh no oh no oh no, his soul cried again. He had left the key in the lock to the attic door! He knew it as surely as he knew his own name.

He grabbed the towel, wrapped it around himself, and carefully inched the bathroom door open. Maybe, just maybe, he could retrieve the key before Whit noticed that it wasn't where it should be.

Mark stuck his head into the hallway and looked to his left, in the direction of Whit's room. The door was open, but the room seemed to be empty. He turned to the right and instantly felt something hot shoot from his stomach and through every nerve ending in his body. The attic door was open.

Mark's jaw dropped, and he wasn't sure whether to scream or cry. He heard footsteps on the stairs. Whit emerged from the stairwell with a stricken look on his face. In his hands were the broken pieces of the Indian head paperweight.

"Do you know anything about this?" Whit asked, his face turning red.

Mark stammered, "It . . . it was an accident!"

"An accident!" Whit countered angrily. "You *sneaked* up there and . . . " His voice trailed off into a low growl.

Mark looked at the carpet, the burning in his stomach getting even hotter.

"Do you know what this was?" Whit asked, his voice now a hoarse whisper.

Mark shook his head, even though he *did* know. Then he changed his mind. "Yes," he said softly.

"It was the only thing he ever made for me," Whit said. The edge of anger gave way to a sorrowful tone.

Mark stared at the carpet. Its pattern twisted and turned like snakes as his eyes filled with tears. His knees felt weak, but they were locked in place. He couldn't move even if he wanted to.

"Just go to bed." Whit strode past Mark, went into his room, and slammed the door.

Mark wasn't sure how long he stood there, but it felt like a very long time.

CHAPTER TEN

Morning Flight

Mark slept fitfully. He seemed to be stuck in a nether-world between dreams and reality. Once, he thought Jerry Whittaker was leaning over his bed. Another time, he suddenly sat upright in his bed without knowing why, only to find that his cheeks were wet with tears. Still later, he thought he found the broken Indian head paperweight under his pillow and panicked because he wasn't sure where to hide the pieces. Then a cadaverous woman pushed open the closet door, shook a bony finger at him, and said, "You shouldn't have gone up to the attic."

I'm going to throw away those comic books at the airport, Mark vowed.

The sun finally rose on yet another cloudy day. Mark was already awake and dressed by the time he heard Whit come out of his room. He listened as Whit passed by— *did he stop outside the door for a moment?* — on his way to the stairs.

When he was sure it was clear, Mark crept out of Jason's room and into Whit's. He placed a note on the pillow. It said "I'm sorry" with Mark's signature underneath. He crept back out again, picked up his case, and walked downstairs. He considered walking out the door and back to his own house, but he realized he wouldn't have a way to the airport, nor did he know how to get his airplane tickets. So he put the case down and walked into the kitchen.

Whit silently laid out breakfast for Mark. Worse than his silence was that Whit wouldn't look at him. Mark wanted to cry all over again. But he didn't. Instead, he simply picked at the ham and eggs.

Mark looked at the clock. 7:45. His flight left at 9:30. The airport was only 15 minutes away, so Mark wondered how they would spend the time. Sitting in this stony silence? *Please, Mr. Whittaker . . . yell at me or something,* Mark thought. *Just don't ignore me like this.*

As if by magic, Whit spoke. "Let's go," he said.

It was a relief for Mark. Maybe Whit would just drop him off at the airport and end their misery.

It rained as they drove, and the hum and swish of the windshield wipers were the only sounds. Mark cleared his throat a couple of times, wanting to say something, but he didn't dare. He began to see signs for the Odyssey Municipal Airport, and his worry increased. *I can't leave Whit like this,* he said to himself. It would be torture. It would ruin his life. A note wasn't enough. He had to apologize out loud. *Now.*

Whit drove into the airport parking lot, pulled a ticket from the machine, and glided into a parking place. An airplane roared overhead.

"Here we are," said Whit.

His voice broke the dam of Mark's emotion. "I'm sorry, Mr. Whittaker," he said. "You don't know how sorry I am! I never should've gone up in the attic. I know that now. I should've listened to you. And I didn't mean to break Jerry's paperweight. It was a stupid accident because I was stupid for being there in the first place, and I'll do anything you want me to do to make it up somehow if I can, but I know I can't, but I'll try if—" Mark's voice was strangled by tears, and he pushed them out with heaving sobs.

Whit raised his hand. "Whoa, hold on," he said.

Mark lowered his head, and Whit gently placed his hand on his shoulder. Mark got control of himself and lifted his eyes. For the first time that morning, he looked Whit full in the face. Whit's eyes were red and puffy as if he'd been crying, too.

"I'm really, really sorry," Mark said again.

Whit managed a smile, but it didn't have its usual brightness. "I know you're sorry, Mark. I know. And I accept that. Okay?"

Mark nodded.

Whit sighed. "I loved Jerry very much. And when he died in Vietnam, I was devastated. It was more than I could take. My whole family was thrown into a very dark time.

"We were living in the Chicago area when it happened. We decided to leave. I suppose we thought we could escape the memories. In a way, we did. We found Odyssey and thought we could start over again."

Whit stared out at the passing cars for a moment. He seemed preoccupied by a man and woman saying good-bye at the curb in front of the terminal. "Odyssey was good for us," he finally continued. "We didn't even buy a house with enough room for Jerry's furniture. It got stored away in the attic. It was our way of saying good-bye to him, I think."

Again Whit paused as the couple at the curb kissed and the woman rushed into the terminal. The man watched her for a moment, then climbed into his car and left.

"After Jenny died, I was heartbroken all over again. But this time Jana and Jason were grown up, so I had to grieve alone. Maybe because she died near me, instead of in a far-away country, I found I could handle it better. But the pain of Jerry's death came back again. One day, I was up in the attic and saw all the furniture from his room. I set it up the way you saw it—a re-creation of the way his room looked when he went off to war. It became my secret place. I was wrong to do it."

"There's nothing wrong with having a hideout," Mark offered.

"This secret place was different, though," Whit replied. "Maybe it was a way to cope with the loss of two loved ones, but I found myself spending a lot of time up there. Just sitting. Remembering. Losing myself in the past. That can be a dangerous thing to do. I wanted things to be the way they used to be."

Mark closed his eyes. Those were familiar words to him; an echo of the feelings he had when he first moved to Odyssey. It took Whit and the Imagination Station to make him realize you can never make things the way they were before.

"Nobody knew about my secret place—until you came along. And I was very angry with you for finding it. It hurt. I resented the intrusion."

"I know, Mr. Whittaker, and I'm sorry. I'll never tell anyone about—"

Again Whit held up his hand for silence. "Last night, after you went to bed, I thought about it and prayed and . . . realized *I* was wrong to get so emotionally tied up in my memories—in Jerry's old life. A life that's gone. It brought back sweet memories, but it brought back pain, too. And loss.

"With that room, I was keeping open the old wounds, not giving them a chance to heal."

"Just like I've been doing with Patti's cast," Mark said, suddenly remembering their conversation the day before.

"Yes, just like that," Whit agreed. "So, I decided that I'm going to dismantle the room."

The announcement took Mark by surprise.

Whit nodded and continued, "It's time to let go of the past and let old wounds heal. And I want to thank you for helping me realize that."

Being thanked for what he did was another surprise for Mark. *I'll never understand adults as long as I live,* he thought. But he was relieved, too. Now they could be friends again.

They picked up Mark's ticket at the airline counter. There was still time to kill, so they went to the airport cafeteria and had some disgusting, watered-down orange juice. Afterward, Mark suddenly remembered one other important detail. While Whit watched him curiously, Mark dug into his case and pulled out the comic books.

"You're kidding," Whit said. "You *read* that trash?"

"Not anymore," Mark said as he dropped them into a nearby trash can.

Whit walked Mark to the gate and—the third big surprise—hugged Mark good-bye just before he boarded the plane.

"Have a good trip, Mark," he whispered.

"Thank you, Mr. Whittaker," Mark replied.

Whit reached into his pocket, produced a small package, and slipped it into Mark's jacket pocket. "Don't look at it until you get to your parents' house," he said.

CHAPTER ELEVEN

Home Away from Home

Something was wrong. Mark knew it instinctively when his mother and father picked him up at National Airport in Washington, D.C. Yeah, they were all smiles and gave him long hugs and asked how the flight was, but it didn't ring true. They seemed tense and ill at ease.

Mark felt deflated. He didn't realize until the plane landed that he had expected his parents to scoop him up in their arms at the gate, announce that all was well, and promise they'd all live happily ever after.

He sank further into disappointment when his mom and dad began to argue during the ride from the airport. Their comments were too adult and veiled for Mark to guess what their problem was, but it was all too familiar. Just like old times. He sank into the thick cushion of the backseat and fingered the mysterious gift Whit had given him.

Mark entered his old home like a stranger. It was the same as he remembered it, but it didn't feel as if it belonged to him anymore. It could have been a next-door neighbor's house for all he cared. *Odyssey is my home*, he realized.

Julie kissed him again and said how glad she was that he was with them. Richard, his father, agreed and added, "Why don't you take your case up to your room?"

Mark did, hoping his old room might spark something within him. It did—but not the feeling he expected. Through the vent, he could hear his parents' voices from down in the kitchen. They were fighting. Mark felt a rush of nausea as he was transported back in time to those mornings and nights in the spring when he played up in his room, hoping to drown out their bitter words. It was happening all over again. Nothing had changed between them. All the counseling and promises and wishful thinking hadn't amounted to anything.

Mark tossed his case on the bed and walked to the window. It perspired as the outside humidity clashed with the air conditioning inside. The familiar scene overlooking his backyard was blurred. Maybe it was the window. Maybe it was the tears that filled his eyes.

He wanted to leave. He wanted to be back in Odyssey

with Whit and Patti. But he wanted both his mother and father to be with him. Together. Was it too much to ask?

For comfort, he reached into his pocket and fingered Whit's gift.

From downstairs, Mark could hear his parents shout about something that happened when they first got married. *That long ago?* Mark wondered. *Why would they fight about that now?*

He decided not to cry anymore. Nor would he leave. Nor would he join their fight. He simply walked down to the kitchen and poured himself a glass of milk. By that time, Julie and Richard had moved their fight to the living room. Once, Julie suggested that they continue their conversation later—"for Mark's sake." That triggered another argument about whether Mark was old enough to understand how adults argue with each other.

"It's nothing to worry about," Richard called in to the kitchen to assure Mark.

Mark shrugged and sipped his milk, then casually took off his jacket and threw it over one of the chairs. The small present from Whit fell out of the pocket. He picked it up and decided that now was a good time to open it. The wrapping paper was off in a flash. Underneath was an oblong box. He took off the cover and looked inside. A smile stretched across his face.

It was the key to Whit's attic door.

Mark clutched it tightly in his hand and held it to his

chest. *I'll find a special place for it,* he thought—somewhere so it would always remind him of what had happened and what he had learned.

Richard and Julie were nose to nose in a renewed shouting match when Mark walked into the living room. Their fight had to do with something Richard had said one night after Mark's third birthday party, which Richard didn't think was any worse than something Julie had said to him during Mark's second-grade Christmas pageant.

Mark stood in the center of the room and watched them quietly. Julie noticed him first and looked at him with a curious expression on her face. Richard, catching on that Julie wasn't listening to him anymore, did the same.

"You know what?" Mark said quietly. "Maybe it's time to let old wounds heal."

Richard and Julie looked at him, then at each other.

Mark slipped the key into his jeans pocket and took another drink of milk.

About the Author

Paul McCusker is producer, writer, and director for the *Adventures in Odyssey* audio series. He is also the author of a variety of popular plays including *The First Church of Pete's Garage*, *Snapshots & Portraits*, and co-author of *Sixty-Second Skits* (with Chuck Bolte).

Other Works by the Author

NOVELS:

Strange Journey Back (Focus on the Family)

High Flyer with a Flat Tire (Focus on the Family)

The Secret Cave of Robinwood (Focus on the Family)

Lights Out at Camp What-a-Nut (Focus on the Family)

INSTRUCTIONAL:

Youth Ministry Comedy & Drama:

Better Than Bathrobes But Not Quite Broadway

  (with Chuck Bolte; Group Books)

PLAYS:

Pap's Place (Lillenas)

A Work in Progress (Lillenas)

Snapshots & Portraits (Lillenas)

Camp W (Contemporary Drama Services)

Family Outings (Lillenas)

The Revised Standard Version of Jack Hill (Baker's Plays)

Catacombs (Lillenas)

The Case of the Frozen Saints (Baker's Plays)

The Waiting Room (Baker's Plays)

A Family Christmas (Contemporary Drama Services)

The First Church of Pete's Garage (Baker's Plays)

Home for Christmas (Baker's Plays)

SKETCH COLLECTIONS:

Sixty-Second Skits (with Chuck Bolte; Group Books)

Void Where Prohibited (Baker's Plays)

Some Assembly Required (Contemporary Drama Services)

Quick Skits & Discussion Starters (with Chuck Bolte; Group Books)

Vantage Points (Lillenas)

Batteries Not Included (Baker's Plays)

Souvenirs (Baker's Plays)

Sketches of Harvest (Baker's Plays)

MUSICALS:

The Meaning of Life & Other Vanities (with Tim Albritton;

  Baker's Plays)

Don't Miss the Next "Adventures in Odyssey" Book!

On this and the following pages, you'll find chapter one of *Lights Out at Camp What-A-Nut*, the next book in the "Adventures in Odyssey" series. We hope you enjoy this preview of this book and will then want to read the rest of the story. Don't miss it!

The banner "Welcome to Odyssey Municipal Airport!" stretched across the airline gate, ready to greet the passengers on the approaching plane. Mark Prescott leaned across his mother's seat to get a clear look out the window. Although the pane was dotted with raindrops from yet another late August storm, he could see the banner and felt his heart leap at the name "Odyssey."

"Are you glad to be back?" Julie, his mother, asked.

Mark nodded.

Julie rubbed Mark's back. "I was just thinking how nice it is to be home again. Funny, huh?—thinking about Odyssey as home."

Mark understood what she meant. When his parents separated the previous June, Mark was sure nothing worse could ever happen to him. That is, until Julie moved Mark to her grandmother's house in Odyssey, halfway across the country from his father, Richard, and their home in Washington, D.C. Then Mark *knew* was the end of the world.

But that was last June.

In the almost three months since then, he had made new friends, enjoyed Odyssey's gentle charm, and taken part in some exciting adventures (including taking a trip in a time machine and solving a mystery). Slowly, Mark felt less like a stranger and more like a welcome friend. By August, it was as if he'd always been there—and always would be.

Mark and Julie followed the crowd of passengers from the plane to the baggage-claim area. A horn sounded a warning blast, and the conveyor belt loudly whirred to life. Mark stood nearby, grabbing their luggage when it came past. They tossed the cases onto a cart and pushed it to the long-term parking area where Julie had parked the car only a few days before.

Only a few days? It seems longer than that, Mark thought, then said so out loud.

"Did it seem long because you didn't enjoy yourself?" Julie asked as she closed the trunk.

"I guess so," Mark said with a shrug. "It wasn't as much fun as I thought it would be. It's like . . . our house wasn't ours anymore."

Julie nodded her head, a lock of her long, brown hair falling across her face. "I understand. Everything looked the same as it did before we left, but it seemed different some-

how. Once or twice, I felt like I was a visitor in a museum."
She started the car and backed out of the parking space.

"All my old friends were either away on vacation or they
didn't want to see me," Mark added. That bothered him a
lot. Somehow it didn't seem fair that they went on with their
lives without him being there to give his approval.

Julie paid the parking attendant, wound up her window,
and pulled away. "That's the hardest part. When you go
away, you think everyone should suddenly stop in their
tracks and never do anything important without you. You
think you're the only one who can change or make new
friends or have new experiences. And when you come back,
it's a shock to find out that their lives kept going—just like
yours did."

"Yeah, but Mike Adams is hanging around Tom Nelson!
They couldn't stand each other before!"

Julie laughed and said, "Just like you never thought you
could have a girl as a friend."

His mom was referring to Patti Eldridge, a girl who had
become Mark's closest friend in Odyssey during the summer.

"That's different," Mark replied. He stared out the passen-
ger window thoughtfully. "And I thought you and Dad . . ."
He glanced down at his lap uncomfortably.

"You thought your dad and I would get back together
again. I know."

She was right. The reason they had gone to Washington,
D.C., in the first place was so that Mark's mom and dad

could iron out their differences. But by the time Richard dropped Mark and Julie off at the airport for their return trip to Odyssey, it was clear that wasn't going to happen.

"I'm sorry, Mark," Julie said. "I really thought your dad and I would work it all out. I thought this trip would be the end of our separation. I know you're disappointed."

"Wars have ended quicker than you two getting back together," Mark said as they drove away from the airport.

Julie smiled wearily in return. "You have to be patient. You may not see the improvements, but they're there."

"Then why aren't we together again?"

"Because we're not ready," she answered. "I won't get back with your father until I'm sure we're ready."

"But that's what you and Dad keep saying!"

"I know. But some things came up in our counseling session that we have to figure out." Julie sighed. "You wouldn't understand."

"What wouldn't I understand?" Mark snapped. "Why do you always think I don't understand?"

Julie glanced at Mark, a pained expression on her face.

"I'm sorry," Mark said. "I didn't mean to be so sharp."

Julie acknowledged the apology with a nod, then reached across the seat to touch Mark's hand. "It's all leading somewhere, Mark. You have to trust us. We've needed this time to mend our wounds."

Mark shot her an ornery look, then said, "Maybe you should buy some Band-Aids."

She pinched him playfully and drove on.